Hudson and the Magic Rope

By: Arthur Raisfeld
Illustrated by: Emily Wilson

To Hudson Dylan Raisfeld - the light of my life.

One day, Hudson went exploring.

He went up hills

and down.

He walked by trees,

and by rivers.

He looked under rocks

and on top of them.
He didn't want to miss anything!

He spotted butterflies,
birds

and once a leaping fish!

As he was walking, he came across a rope.

He looked around for the rope's owner, but didn't see anyone.
He looked on the rope for a name, but nothing was there.

Hudson got tired.
"Gee," he thought, "I wish I had a chair to sit in."

Suddenly, the rope turned into a chair.
"Wow," Hudson thought, "the rope must be magic!"

"What a great thing to have!"
Hudson thought.

He walked along the river's edge with his magic
rope. On the other side of the fast moving water was
a family playing with a cute puppy. The puppy barked
and started to chase a butterfly.

Just then, the puppy fell into the water.
"Oh no!" Hudson shouted.
The puppy couldn't swim and the current was
carrying him faster than anyone could run.

Hudson knew that if he threw the magic rope he could save the puppy but he would probably never see his fabulous rope again!

Hudson went home, still worried about the puppy.

He went to sleep worried.

The next morning at breakfast, Hudson's dad was reading the local paper. Inside, there was a picture of the puppy! "What does that story say, Daddy?" asked Hudson excitedly.

"Missing puppy returned to worried family,"
said his dad.

Hudson smiled all day.

Made in the USA
Lexington, KY
28 April 2018